Copyright © 2017 by Nikki Maloney

Printed in the United States

ISBN-13: 978-1539453222

ISBN-10: 1539453227

LCCN: 2017904952

CreateSpace Independent Publishing Platform, North Charleston, SC

First Printing, July 2017

For information contact:
www.nikkimaloney.com

For more titles in this series, please visit: **www.amazon.com**

The Peppermints: A Ski Vacation

The Peppermints: Summer Camp Treasury

The Peppermints: Thanksgiving Day Parade

The Peppermints: Be Careful What You Wish For

The Peppermints: Big Sur

The *Peppermints*

A TRIP TO THE ZOO

story by

Nikki Maloney

illustrated by

Christian Ridder

"There are two good things in life –
freedom of thought and freedom of action."

-W. Somerset Maugham

To Goodie, for the gift of the Peppermints and
to his father Frank, the original storyteller,
who always told the truth.

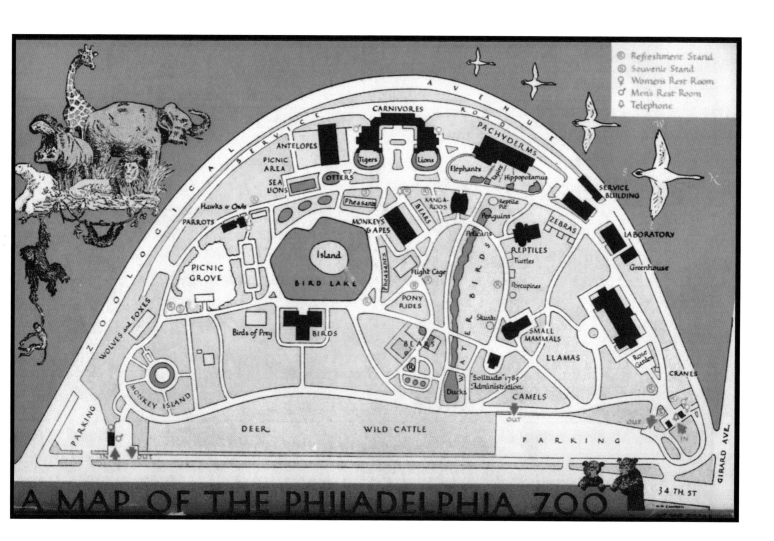

A MAP OF THE PHILADELPHIA ZOO

Every April, the Peppermint family climbed into the old station wagon and headed to Philadelphia. As they traveled south, Mrs. Peppermint found pleasure in the changing seasons.

Out the window there were vivid signs of an emerging spring: buds about to burst from tree limbs, spring peepers popping up alongside the highway, and the sun, which seemed to intensify with every passing half-hour. It was like boarding a rollercoaster and slowly climbing the first incline. Spring was coming, coming, coming and then, whoosh, it was undeniably there.

Once off the highway, Mr. Peppermint weaved through the Main Line and then worked his way down Route 1. Continuing on, he drove through Fairmount Park past Memorial Hall.

Mrs. Peppermint loved to see the forsythia bushes in full bloom with their electric yellow flowers accenting the centennial buildings lining the street.

Crossing Girard Avenue onto 34th Street, the Peppermint children gazed out the window catching a glimpse of their destination. To the right, Pete peered at the statue positioned outside the entrance while Patty admired the prominent, black, wrought iron gates.

Peggy praised the two ornate Victorian gatehouses that stood like guardians on either side of the main entrance, and Philpot stretched his neck glancing upward at the towering sycamore trees that lined the street between the Schuylkill River and the Zoological Garden.

Mrs. Peppermint remembered visiting America's first zoo when she was a little girl. She recalled her father informing her that on July 1, 1874, three thousand people walked or rode in trolleys or horse-drawn carriages to celebrate opening day. She learned that many visitors traveled from downtown Philadelphia up the Schuylkill River by steamboat. They would unload at the zoo's own wharf.

When Mrs. Peppermint shared her memory, Patty imagined herself in the olden days disembarking the splendid steamer onto the landing.

Presently, Mr. Peppermint turned into the south lot and parked the car. The children piled out and rushed to the ticket window. Once admitted, the family entered through the heavy turnstiles, descended the stairs, and there in front of them stood Monkey Island.

Philpot patrolled the primates as they playfully chased one another around the rock formation. Pete applauded the chimpanzee's dexterity as he observed one chimp grabbing hold of a ring that was hanging from a metal bar with one hand while reaching for another ring that was in motion with the other.

Peggy detected movement on the other side of the rocks and strained to see the action taking place. Her patience was rewarded when she discovered two young chimps taking turns dangling from a jungle gym. Peggy pictured herself in her backyard hanging from the top of her swing set from her knees.

Jolting Peggy out of her thoughts, Patty summoned her family to move on, so she could pay a visit to her favorite mammals. Strolling by the picnic grove, the family curved around the crescent- shaped walkway past the parrots, hawks, and owls.

Approaching the otter exhibit, Patty informed her sister and brothers, "Did you know that a family of otters is called a romp, while a group of otters in the water is a called a raft?"

The children surveyed two otters swimming swiftly side by side on their backs while the other otters took turns slithering down an embankment creating their own slide. Patty tracked one otter swimming from one side of the pond to the other. When it reached the far side, the creature did a graceful flip then turned over and pushed off the wall to return to the other side. Patty considered her own attempts to master a flip turn during last summer's swim season.

After some time, Pete urged everyone to advance, and soon they came upon the lions and tigers. Pete regarded the magnificent carnivores strolling right in front of him. The big cats lumbered slowly around the pen or rested in the shade of the low lying trees.

Potty asked, "Pete, why are the lions so sleepy?"

Pete answered, "Lions and tigers are nocturnal. In the wild, the big cats hunt all through the night, and they can spend up to twenty hours a day sleeping and relaxing."

Excited to see the pachyderms, Peggy prodded her family toward the elephants. Peggy held a deep fondness for the elegant giants, and wondered, with their remarkable memories if they remembered her visit from last year.

Standing next to Peggy, Potty reached into his pants pocket and pulled out a few gumdrops. As he lifted them up to his mouth, one of the elephants glanced in his direction, lifted its trunk up in the air, and swayed, moving it side to side. Potty minded the motion of the elephant's trunk and thought of his little league team and the fluid swing of a baseball bat.

The Peppermints threaded their way along the path and came upon the hippo's pen. Peggy was astonished that an enormous creature would have such tiny ears. When one of the hippos yawned, Patty could not believe how big their mouths were and how sharp their bottom fangs seemed.

Pete attended the animals and shared with his sisters that he had read an article in last month's *National Geographic* magazine that stated, "Hippos are also referred to as river horses."

Pete watched the massive creatures swim in their pond and counted while the hippos went under water. Pete recalled when he broke the pool record for holding his breath for fifty seconds and stood in awe as the hippos held their breath for almost six minutes!

Pete noticed that while two of the hippos wrestled with one another in the watering hole, a lone hippo wandered around on land, walking slow and looking miserable. Pointing out the animal, Potty came over to take a closer look.

Potty said, "Pete, look at that. That hippo looks sad and lonely. Is he pouting? See how his bottom lip sticks out. I think we should call him Lippy, Lippy the Hippy!"

Suddenly, Potty had an idea. He reached into his pants pocket, pulled out another gumdrop, and hurled it with all his might. It soared through the air and bounced on the ground landing right under the creature's nose. The hippo smelled around, located the strange object, and scooped it up with his lips.

Several seconds passed and what appeared to be a smile spread across the hippo's face, and he turned in the direction from where the treat came.

Potty called out, "Lippy, Lippy! Over here! I have more treats for you."

Lippy slowly meandered over past the watering hole and approached the steel fence. He seemed to be having a hard time locating Potty. One of the zookeepers came over and explained that the hippo was quite old, and his eyesight was failing.

Presently, a loud noise surprised the Peppermint family, and they looked around for an answer as to what it could be. Patty noticed that the zookeeper had an exasperated look on his face. He informed the Peppermints that the sound was the fire siren. Apparently there was a fire in the zoo, and everyone had to be evacuated immediately.

Mrs. Peppermint gathered the children, and the family walked briskly toward the front entrance. Along the way, Patty observed several animals causing a commotion. She felt they knew something was terribly wrong.

"What will they do with all the animals, Mother?" Patty asked out of breath.

Mrs. Peppermint calmed Patty down saying, "I am sure they have a plan to get all the animals to safety dear; now let us do what the zookeeper said and head for the closest exit."

By the time they reached the front entrance, hundreds of concerned individuals stood just outside the main gate. There were so many people that the crowd stretched down Girard Avenue.

Once on the other side of the gate, the Peppermints looked back in and saw huge plumes of smoke engulfing the zoo. One gentleman held the new *TR 63* transistor radio and listened as the mayor alerted everyone about the fire and informed his listeners that people were currently being evacuated.

Concerned, Pete asked, "What about the animals, Father?"

Mr. Peppermint assured Pete that the zoo officials had an emergency plan, and they would do everything in their power to chaperone the animals to safety.

Just then, Potty thought about Lippy. He was sure the other animals would follow their handlers out of the zoo, but how could Lippy, with being blind and so old. He would never make it out. Potty felt strongly that he had to do something.

He broke away from the crowd and dashed into the zoo. Right away, a firefighter caught Potty and demanded that he go back to his parents. Potty explained the emergency situation.

A nearby zookeeper overheard their conversation and because the fire had not reached the hippo pen, he agreed to take the firefighter and Potty to the hippos.

When they arrived, the two hippos that were in the water had followed the zookeepers out of the pen and into the alley behind the zoo. But there stood Lippy, lip jutted out, looking frightened and anxious.

Potty called out to Lippy, and Lippy turned in his direction.

"I have more treats for you, boy," said Potty.

Lippy just stood there. Then the zookeeper noted that the animal headed toward the safety of the water, just as he would do in the wild. Observing the hippo's behavior, Potty asked permission to go into the pen. Knowing they were running out of time, the zookeeper took Potty by the hand and led him right up next to the hippo. Lippy swung his head around and nearly knocked Potty down. Then Lippy proceeded to sniff at Potty's pocket.

Reaching into his pocket, Potty pronounced, "Is this what you want boy?" And he presented the delectable gumdrop.

Potty held out his hand, and Lippy lapped up the candy. Then Potty put a gumdrop in his hand, placed his hand directly in front of Lippy's nose, then lowered the sweet treat to the ground. The hippo followed, and once Potty released the candy, Lippy devoured it.

Potty backed up a couple feet and did the same thing. Lippy wheeled around and trailing behind Potty, he ate the gumdrops along the way. Potty was running low on candy, so he stretched out the distance between the bonbons a little farther each time, and before he knew it, Lippy was out of the pen and onto the walkway.

The fire was raging now, and the smoke was wafting steadily in their direction. Potty recognized he had to make a change of plans if they were going to make it out unharmed. He reached into his back pocket and pulled out his baseball, an old safety pin, and the last gumdrop he had. He pulled the string out of the ball and yelled for the zookeeper to pull off a long piece of bamboo from the gate. Potty tied the string to the end of the piece of bamboo and secured it with a knot.

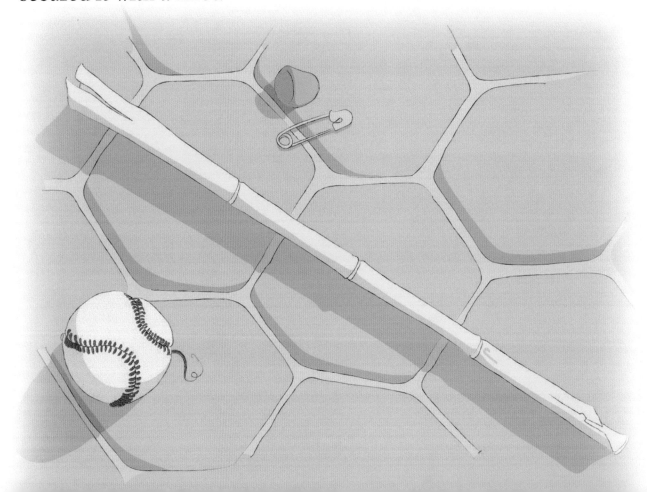

Then he took the safety pin and pierced a hole in the gumdrop and attached the safety pin to the bottom of the string. It looked just like a fishing pole, but instead of a worm, the bait was a gumdrop.

He asked the zookeeper to give him a leg up onto Lippy, and Potty climbed aboard the animal's back. He held out the rod above Lippy's nose. Lippy took a big sniff, wiggled his ears, and opened his mouth wide attempting to get the gumdrop. Potty encouraged Lippy to get the sweet treat, which propelled the animal forward.

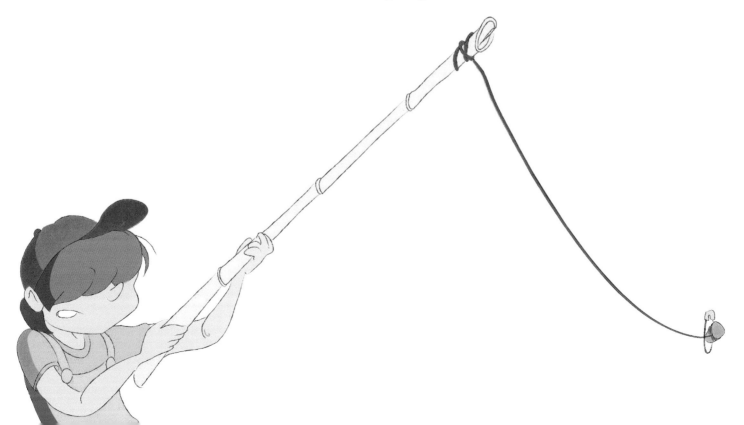

By now, every television station was covering the event. Reporters were interviewing citizens about the fire at the zoo. A reporter was talking with the Peppermints, who were explaining how Potty had gone back into the zoo with the firefighter and the zookeeper to save the hippo.

Just then, through the smoke emerged the firefighter and the zookeeper flanking the enormous hippo, who sauntered toward the front gate. And there, atop the creature was Potty, holding the stick in one hand and waving to the crowd with the other.

People went bananas. Pete started to cheer, "Lippy, Lippy, Lippy!" And soon everyone joined in.

The firefighter received word that all the people and animals had been safely evacuated. After the firefighter helped Potty down off Lippy, the animal turned in Potty's direction with a big smile as if to say *thank you*.

The Peppermints raced over to give Potty a big hug. Then the mayor approached the family and thanked Potty for his bravery.

Potty responded casually, "Aw it was nothin'. My Dad always taught me to never leave a man behind."

Mr. Peppermint said, "Uh, Potty, in this case, it's never leave a hippo behind."

Everyone laughed and clapped for Potty.

The End

Read this story again!

There are 32 peppermint sticks hidden in the pages of the story. The shape of the peppermint sticks should look like the shapes below:

For a helpful guide to find all the hidden peppermint sticks and to discover more titles, visit **nikkimaloney.com**

**I want to express my heartfelt thanks
to the following people:**

To Mom and Dad, Fran, Chrissy, and Tim, I am blessed to be part of
such an incredible family.

To Steve: for your friendship and love *no matter what.*

To Alec, Sean and Tatum: my eternal source of inspiration. Thank
you for remembering the little details.

To my friends and family, your support and shared enthusiasm kept
me motivated throughout the writing process.

To the adult readers and young listeners, especially those at
Gladwyne Elementary and Wenonah Elementary,
for their excitement and honest opinions.

To Dr. Murphy, truly one of the most generous people I've ever met.
Your wisdom and encouragement have given me something I can
never repay. I am forever grateful.

To the many teachers and students from whom I have learned. You
all inhabit a special place in my heart.

To Heide, my strong, beautiful, intelligent, and resourceful friend.
You always take the time to give things a second look and are willing
to battle over a comma.

Lastly, to Christian Ridder, an outstanding artist and extraordinary
human being, for reimagining *The Peppermints* and approaching things
from an original perspective.

About the Author

Nikki Maloney has enjoyed writing since attending her first poetry workshop at Fairfield Woods Library in Connecticut. She currently works as a reading specialist, and lives in Pennsylvania with her husband, three children, two dogs and guinea pig. This is her sixth children's book.

About the Illustrator

Christian Ridder has been drawing and painting all his life. He only began painting seriously in high school. He currently studies architecture in Philadelphia and hopes to incorporate what he loves about the past into the art and architecture of the future. This is what gives the nostalgic setting of *The Peppermints* such an appeal to him.

visit the **ZOO**

PHILADELPHIA

Federal Art Project, W. P. A. Pennsylvania

Made in the USA
Columbia, SC
12 October 2017